Eeyore Has
a Birthday

A. A. Milne
Illustrated by E. H. Shepard

METHUEN

Eeyore, the old grey Donkey, stood by the side of the stream, and looked at himself in the water.

'Pathetic,' he said. 'That's what it is. Pathetic.'

He turned and walked slowly down the stream for twenty yards, splashed across it, and walked slowly back on the other side. Then he looked at himself in the water again.

'As I thought,' he said. 'No better from *this* side. But nobody minds.

Nobody cares.
Pathetic, that's
what it is.'

There was a
crackling noise
in the bracken
behind him, and
out came Pooh.

'Good morning, Eeyore,' said Pooh.

'Good morning, Pooh Bear,' said
Eeyore gloomily. 'If it *is* a good
morning,' he said. 'Which I doubt,'

said he.

'Why, what's the matter?'

'Nothing, Pooh Bear, nothing. We can't all, and some of us don't. That's all there is to it.'

'Can't all *what*?' said Pooh, rubbing his nose.

'Gaiety. Song-and-dance. Here we go round the mulberry bush.'

'Oh!' said Pooh. He thought for a long time, and then asked, 'What mulberry bush is that?'

'Bon-hommy,' went on Eeyore gloomily. 'French word meaning bonhommy,' he explained. 'I'm not complaining, but There It Is.'

Pooh sat down on a large stone, and tried to think this out. It sounded to him like a riddle, and he was never much good at riddles, being a Bear of Very Little Brain. So he sang

Cottleston Pie

instead:

Cottleston, Cottleston, Cottleston Pie,

A fly can't bird, but a bird can fly.

Ask me a riddle and I reply:

'Cottleston, Cottleston, Cottleston Pie.'

That was the first verse. When he had finished it, Eeyore didn't actually say that he didn't like it, so Pooh very kindly sang the second verse to him:

Cottleston, Cottleston, Cottleston Pie,

A fish can't whistle and neither can I.

Ask me a riddle and I reply:

'Cottleston, Cottleston, Cottleston Pie.'

Eeyore still said nothing at all, so Pooh hummed the third verse quietly to himself:

Cottleston, Cottleston, Cottleston Pie,

Why does a chicken, I don't know why.

Ask me a riddle and I reply:

'Cottleston, Cottleston, Cottleston Pie.'

'That's right,' said Eeyore. 'Sing.
Umty-tiddly, umty-too. Here we
go gathering Nuts and May. Enjoy
yourself.'

'I am,' said Pooh.

'Some can,' said Eeyore.

'Why, what's the matter?'

'*Is* anything the matter?'

'You seem so sad, Eeyore.'

'Sad? Why should I be sad? It's my birthday. The happiest day of the year.'

'Your birthday?'

said Pooh in great surprise.

'Of course it is. Can't you see? Look at all the presents I have had.' He waved a foot from side to side. 'Look at the birthday cake. Candles and pink sugar.'

Pooh looked – first to the right and then to the left.

'Presents?' said Pooh. 'Birthday cake?' said Pooh. '*Where*?'

'Can't you see them?'

'No,' said Pooh.

'Neither can I,' said Eeyore. 'Joke,' he explained. 'Ha ha!'

Pooh scratched his head, being a little puzzled by all this.

'But is it really your birthday?' he asked.

'It is.'

'Oh! Well, many happy returns of the day, Eeyore.'

'And many happy returns to you, Pooh Bear.'

'But it isn't *my* birthday.'

'No, it's mine.'

'But you said "Many happy returns"—'

'Well, why not? You don't always want to be miserable on my birthday, do you?'

'Oh I see,' said Pooh.

'It's bad enough,' said Eeyore, almost breaking down, 'being miserable myself, what with no presents and no cake and no candles, and no proper notice taken of me at all, but if everybody else is going to be miserable too—'

This was too much for Pooh. 'Stay there!' he called to Eeyore, as he turned and hurried back home as quick as he could; for he felt that he must get poor Eeyore a present of *some* sort at once, and he could always think of a proper one afterwards.

Outside his house he found Piglet, jumping up and down trying to reach the knocker.

'Hallo, Piglet,' he said.

'Hallo, Pooh,' said Piglet.

'What are *you* trying to do?'

'I was trying to reach the knocker,' said Piglet. 'I just came round—'

'Let me do it for you,' said Pooh kindly. So he reached up and knocked at the door. 'I have just seen Eeyore,' he began, 'and poor Eeyore is in a Very Sad Condition, because it's his birthday, and nobody has taken any notice of it, and he's very Gloomy – you know what

Eeyore is – and there he was, and—
What a long time whoever lives here
is answering this door.' And he

knocked again.

'But, Pooh,' said Piglet, 'it's
your own house!'

'Oh!' said Pooh. 'So it is,' he
said. 'Well, let's go in.'

So in they went. The first thing Pooh
did was to go to the cupboard to see if
he had quite a small jar of honey left;
and he had, so he took it down.

'I'm giving this to Eeyore,' he explained, 'as a present. What are *you* going to give?'

'Couldn't I give it too?' said Piglet. 'From both of us?'

'No,' said Pooh. 'That would *not* be a good plan.'

'All right, then, I'll give him a balloon. I've got one left from my party. I'll go and get it now, shall I?'

'That, Piglet, is a *very* good idea. It is just what Eeyore wants to cheer him up. Nobody can be uncheered with a balloon.'

So off Piglet trotted; and in the other direction went Pooh, with his jar of honey.

It was a warm day, and he had a long way to go. He hadn't gone more than half-way when a sort of funny feeling began to creep all over him. It began at the tip of his nose and trickled all through him and out at the soles of his feet. It was just as if somebody inside him were saying, 'Now then, Pooh, time for a little something.'

'Dear, dear,' said Pooh, 'I didn't know it was as late as that.' So he sat down and took the top off his jar of honey. 'Lucky I brought this with me,' he thought. 'Many a bear going out on a warm day like this would never have thought of bringing a little something with him.' And he began to eat.

'Now let me see,' he thought, as he took his

last lick of the inside of the jar, 'where was I going? Ah, yes, Eeyore.' He got up slowly.

And then, suddenly, he remembered. He had eaten Eeyore's birthday present!

'*Bother!*'

said Pooh.
'What *shall*
I do? I *must* give
him *something*.'

For a little while he couldn't think of anything. Then he thought: 'Well, it's a very nice pot, even if there's no honey in it, and if I washed it clean, and got somebody to write "*A Happy Birthday*" on it, Eeyore could keep things in it, which might be Useful.' So, as he was just passing the Hundred Acre Wood, he went inside to call on Owl, who lived there.

'Good morning, Owl,' he said.

'Good morning, Pooh,' said Owl.

'Many happy returns
of Eeyore's birthday,' said
Pooh.

'Oh, is that what it is?'

'What are you giving him, Owl?'

'What are *you* giving him, Pooh?'

'I'm giving him a Useful Pot to Keep
Things In, and I wanted to ask you—'

'Is this it?' said Owl, taking it out
of Pooh's paw.

'Yes, and I wanted to ask you—'

'Somebody has been keeping

honey in it,' said Owl.

'You can keep *anything* in it,' said Pooh earnestly. 'It's Very Useful like that. And I wanted to ask you—'

'You ought to write "A Happy Birthday" on it.'

'*That* was what I wanted to ask you,' said Pooh. 'Because my spelling is Wobbly. It's good spelling but it Wobbles, and the letters get in the wrong places. Would *you* write "A Happy Birthday" on it for me?'

'It's a nice pot,' said Owl, looking at it all round. 'Couldn't I give it too? From both of us?'

'No,' said Pooh. 'That would *not* be a good plan. Now I'll just wash it first, and then you can write on it.'

Well, he washed the pot out, and dried it, while Owl licked the end of his pencil, and wondered how to spell 'birthday'.

'Can you read, Pooh?' he asked a little anxiously. 'There's a notice about knocking and ringing outside my door, which Christopher Robin wrote. Could you read it?'

'Christopher Robin told me what it said, and *then* I could.'

'Well, I'll tell you what *this* says, and then you'll be able to.'

So Owl wrote . . . and this is what he wrote:

HIPY PAPY BTHUTHDTH
THU THDA BTHUTHDY.

Pooh looked on admiringly.

'I'm just saying "A Happy Birthday",' said Owl carelessly.

'It's a nice long one,' said Pooh, very much impressed by it.

'Well, *actually*, of course, I'm saying "A Very Happy Birthday with love from Pooh." Naturally it takes a good deal of pencil to say a long thing like that.'

'Oh, I see,' said Pooh.

While all this was happening, Piglet had gone back to his own house to get

Eeyore's balloon. He held it
very tightly against himself,
so that it shouldn't blow
away, and he ran as fast as
he could so as to get to Eeyore before
Pooh did; for he thought that he would
like to be the first one to give a present,
just as if he had thought of it without
being told by anybody. And running
along, and thinking how pleased
Eeyore would be, he didn't look where
he was going . . .

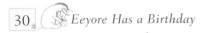

and suddenly he put his foot in a rabbit hole, and fell down flat on his face.

Piglet lay there, wondering what had happened. At first he thought that the whole world had blown up; and then he thought that perhaps only the Forest part of it had; and then he thought that

perhaps only *he* had, and he was now
alone in the moon or somewhere, and
would never see Christopher Robin or
Pooh or Eeyore again. And then he
thought, 'Well, even if I'm in the moon,
I needn't be face downwards all the time,'
so he got cautiously up and looked
about him.

He was still in the Forest!

'Well, that's funny,' he thought.
'I wonder what that bang was. I couldn't
have made such a noise just falling down.

And where's my balloon? And what's that small piece of damp rag doing?'

 It was the

balloon!

'Oh, dear!' said Piglet. 'Oh, dear, oh, dearie, dearie, dear! Well, it's too late now. I can't go back, and I haven't another balloon, and perhaps Eeyore doesn't *like* balloons so *very* much.'

So he trotted on, rather sadly now, and down he came to the side of the stream where Eeyore was, and called out to him.

'Good morning, Eeyore,' shouted Piglet.

'Good morning, Little Piglet,' said Eeyore. 'If it *is* a good morning,' he said. 'Which I doubt,' said he. 'Not that it matters,' he said.

'Many happy returns of the day,' said Piglet, having now got closer.

Eeyore stopped looking at himself in the stream, and turned to stare at Piglet.

'Just say that again,' he said.

'Many hap—'

'Wait a moment.'

Balancing on three legs, he began to bring his fourth leg very cautiously up to his ear. 'I did this yesterday,' he explained, as he fell down for the third time. 'It's quite easy. It's so as I can hear better . . . There, that's done it! Now then, what were you saying?' He pushed his ear forward with his hoof.

'Many happy returns of the day,' said Piglet again.

'Meaning me?'

'Of course, Eeyore.'

'My birthday?'

'Yes.'

'Me having a real birthday?'

'Yes, Eeyore, and I've brought you a present.'

Eeyore took down his right hoof from his right ear, turned round, and with great difficulty put up his left hoof.

'I must have that in the other ear,' he said. 'Now then.'

'A present,' said Piglet very loudly.

'Meaning me again?'

'Yes.'

'My birthday still?'

'Of course, Eeyore.'

'Me going on having a real birthday?'

'Yes, Eeyore, and I brought you a balloon.'

'*Balloon*?' said Eeyore. 'You did say balloon? One of those big coloured things you blow up? Gaiety, song-and-dance, here we are and there we are?'

'Yes, but I'm afraid – I'm very sorry,

Eeyore – but when I was running along to bring it you, I fell down.'

'Dear, dear, how unlucky! You ran too fast, I expect. You didn't hurt yourself, Little Piglet?'

'No, but I – I – oh, Eeyore, I burst the balloon!'

There was a very long silence.

*   *   *

'My balloon?' said Eeyore at last. Piglet nodded.

'My birthday balloon?'

'Yes, Eeyore,' said Piglet, sniffing a little. 'Here it is. With – with many happy returns of the day.' And he gave Eeyore the small piece of damp rag.

'Is this it?' said Eeyore, a little surprised. Piglet nodded.

'My present?'

Piglet nodded again.

'The balloon?'

'Yes.'

'Thank you, Piglet,' said Eeyore. 'You don't mind my asking,' he went on, 'but what colour was this balloon when it – when it *was* a balloon?'

'Red.'

'I just wondered . . . Red,' he murmured to himself. 'My favourite colour . . . How big was it?'

'About as big as me.'

'I just wondered . . . About as big as Piglet,' he said to himself sadly. 'My favourite size. Well, well.'

Piglet felt very miserable, and didn't know what to say.

He was still opening his mouth to begin something, and then deciding that it wasn't any good saying *that*, when he heard a shout from the other side of the river, and there was Pooh.

'Many happy returns of the day,'
called out Pooh, forgetting that he had
said it already.

'Thank you, Pooh, I'm having them,'
said Eeyore gloomily.

'I've brought you a little present,' said
Pooh excitedly.

'I've had it,' said Eeyore.

Pooh had now splashed across the
stream to Eeyore, and Piglet was sitting
a little way off, his head in his paws,
snuffling to himself.

'It's a Useful Pot,' said
Pooh. 'Here it is. And it's
got "A Very Happy
Birthday with love
from Pooh" written on
it. That's what all that

writing is. And it's for putting things
in. There!'

When Eeyore saw the pot, he became
quite excited.

'Why!' he said. 'I believe my Balloon
will just go into that Pot!'

'Oh, no, Eeyore,' said Pooh.
'Balloons are much too big to go into
Pots. What you do with a balloon is,
you hold the balloon—'

'Not mine,' said Eeyore proudly.
'Look, Piglet!' And as Piglet looked
sorrowfully round, Eeyore picked
the balloon up with his teeth, and
placed it carefully in the pot; picked
it out and put it on the ground; and
then picked it up again and put it
carefully back.

'So it does!' said Pooh.
'It goes in!'

'So it does!' said Piglet.
'And it comes out!'

'Doesn't it?' said Eeyore. 'It
goes in and out like anything.'

'I'm very glad,' said Pooh happily,
'that I thought of giving you a Useful
Pot to put things in.'

'I'm very glad,' said Piglet happily,
'that I thought of giving you
Something to put in a Useful Pot.'

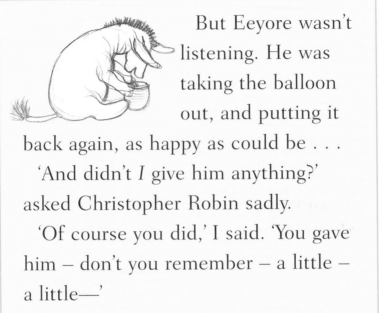

But Eeyore wasn't listening. He was taking the balloon out, and putting it back again, as happy as could be . . .

'And didn't *I* give him anything?' asked Christopher Robin sadly.

'Of course you did,' I said. 'You gave him – don't you remember – a little – a little—'

'I gave him a box of paints to paint things with.'

'That was it.'

'Why didn't I give it to him in the morning?'

'You were so busy getting his party ready for him. He had a cake with icing on the top, and three candles, and his name in pink sugar, and—'

'Yes, *I* remember,' said Christopher Robin.

Eeyore Has a Birthday
is taken from *Winnie-the-Pooh*
originally published in
Great Britain 14 October 1926
by Methuen & Co. Ltd.
Text by A.A. Milne and line drawings by Ernest H. Shepard
copyright under the Berne Convention.

This edition published in Great Britain 2001
by Methuen Children's Books,
an imprint of Egmont Children's Books Limited,
a division of Egmont Holding Limited,
239 Kensington High Street, London W8 6SA.

3   5   7   9   10   8   6   4

Printed in China

ISBN 0 416 19958 5